MW01043498

CURLY AND THE FENT

A Random House book
Published by Random House Australia Pty Ltd
Level 3, 100 Pacific Highway, North Sydney NSW 2060
www.randomhouse.com.au

First published by Random House Australia in 2008

Text copyright © Sally Morgan, Ambelin Kwaymullina, Blaze Kwaymullina and Ezekiel
Kwaymullina 2008
Illustrations copyright © Adam Hill 2008

The moral rights of the authors and the illustrator have been asserted.

All rights reserved. No part of this book may be reproduced or transmitted by any person or
entity, including internet search engines or retailers, in any form or by any means, electronic
or mechanical, including photocopying (except under the statutory exceptions provisions of
the Australian Copyright Act 1968), recording, scanning or by any information storage and
retrieval system without the prior written permission of Random House Australia.

Addresses for companies within the Random House Group can be found at
www.randomhouse.com.au/offices.

National Library of Australia
Cataloguing-in-Publication Entry

> Morgan, Sally.
> Curly and the Fent / authors, Sally Morgan . . . [et al.];
>   illustrator, Adam Hill, 1970–.
>
> 978 1 74166 292 4 (pbk.).
>
> Series: Curly and the Fent; no. 1.
>
> Target audience: For primary school students.
> Subjects: Bullying – Fiction.
>
> A823.3

Cover and internal illustrations by Adam Hill
Cover and internal design by Astred Hicks, Wide Open Media
Typeset in Trade Gothic by Astred Hicks, Wide Open Media, Australia
Printed and bound by The SOS Print + Media Group

Random House Australia uses papers that are natural, renewable and recyclable products
and made from wood grown in sustainable forests. The logging and manufacturing processes
are expected to conform to the environmental regulations of the country of origin.

10 9 8 7 6 5 4 3 2

**Sally Morgan
and Ambelin, Blaze
and Ezekiel Kwaymullina**

illustrated by Adam Hill

RANDOM HOUSE AUSTRALIA

CHAPTER 1

NOISES IN THE DARK

It's the noise that wakes me. A noise that doesn't have any place in a house where everyone is asleep. I open my eyes slowly, straining my ears to catch the sound, but everything is still and quiet. I lie silently for a while, waiting. Crickets are chirruping outside, but that's all. *Must be the cat next door, going for his midnight prowl.* Yawning, I close my eyes again. And that's when I hear it – 'Crrreeeeaaaak.'

That's not a cricket! I'm scared now. My heart beats faster. Slipping a little deeper under my doona, I peer out into the moonlit darkness. Is something hiding in the shadows? I look around carefully. Everything seems all right. Nothing moves, and there are no more sounds. I let out the breath I am holding. *There's nothing there.* Then I hear it again.

'Creeeeeeaaaak.'

The door of my wardrobe opens itself. A single eye is staring out at me.

'MUUMM!' I scream at the top of my lungs.

The wardrobe door slams shut.

Mum stumbles in, tripping over all my junk on the floor. The light bulb has blown, so she can't turn it on.

'What is it, Curly?' she demands.

'What's wrong?'

'There's something in the wardrobe!'

There is silence. Mum is annoyed – I can feel her rolling her eyes in the darkness.

'Besides clothes?' she finally asks.

'A one-eyed beast!' I say fearfully.

Mum sighs. 'Curly, you're eight. That's too old to believe in monsters.'

'But it was looking at me!'

'Remember the time a werewolf was trying to break in through your window?'

That's the trouble with parents; they never forget your most embarrassing mistakes. It wasn't my fault the cat next door casts a very large shadow.

'It's not another werewolf, is it, Curly?' she asks wearily.

'It's real this time, Mum,' I protest. But it sounds weak, even to me.

Had I really seen an eye, or had I just imagined it?

'There's nothing for you to worry about,' Mum reassures me, walking over to the wardrobe. 'Here, I'll show you.'

'Be careful!'

She flings open the door. A pile of my dirty laundry launches itself into the air and collapses on her head. She glares at me from beneath a pair of red underpants. I can't help it, I giggle.

'It's the middle of the night,' Mum growls, 'and you wake me up to play a trick? I have to work tomorrow, Curly,' she reminds me, pulling the underpants off her head and dropping them on the floor. 'That food on the table doesn't just magically appear.'

I feel guilty. I know Mum works hard. Dad does his best, too, but he doesn't live with us any more.

'There was something in there, Mum, really.'

She doesn't believe me. She closes my wardrobe door with a thud.

'It's just your imagination working overtime again, Curly. Go to sleep.'

Mum goes back down the hall to her own room. I lie quietly in the dark. Maybe she is right. Maybe I did imagine it. Or maybe it was just a dream, and I woke up and thought it was real.

'Creeeeeeaaaak!'

The wardrobe door has opened again,

wider this time. Now there are two small eyes gleaming at me in the night.

'I like tricks,' a voice whispers. 'I like them a lot. *Curly.*'

CHAPTER 2

THE MONSTER SLAYER

I don't know what to do. If I shout out now, Mum won't come.

'Hehehe,' the voice says.

In a burst of bravery, I leap out of bed and dive through the dark for my baseball bat.

'Are you a slayer of evil monsters?' the voice asks nervously.

'Yes, I am!' I snap. I crouch down with the bat, ready to swing.

'Oh good!' The voice sounds relieved. 'Because I'm not an evil monster. I'm a Fent.'

I feel surprise. 'What's a Fent?' I ask without thinking.

'Do you want to see?'

Did I? What if it was some kind of trick? What if I saw something scary?

'Point your bat at the wardrobe,' the Fent encourages.

Should I? I just got it for Christmas. What if the Fent makes it explode or something?

Without me doing anything at all, the bat points itself towards the wardrobe and starts to glow like a lightsabre from the *Star Wars* movies.

In a flash something jumps out and lands on the floor. Standing in the light is a short, round, feathery creature with two large, pointy, hairy ears and big feet.

I feel betrayed. 'You *are* a monster!'

'Not a monster, a Fent.' It stares at me, its black eyes wide. 'You're huge!'

I try to imagine what it is seeing – a boy with brown skin, brown eyes, curly black hair and striped pyjamas. I suppose I do look huge to him.

'A Fent. Where do you come from then?'

'Fent Land.'

Well, I guess that makes sense. 'How did you get here?'

'I don't know.' He hangs his head. 'I think I'm lost.'

I feel a bit sorry for him. I got lost once when I was younger. It was in the chocolate

aisle at the supermarket. By the time Mum found me I'd eaten six boxes of Roses chocolates. I was sick for a week afterwards.

'Is that why you hid in my wardrobe?'

He nods. 'Can I sleep in there?'

I put my bat down slowly. The Fent looks so pathetic that I don't want to kick him out. He's so small – what if a dog got him? Killer next door would eat him for dinner.

'Okay,' I agree. 'Just for tonight.'

'Thank you, Curly!'

He dives back inside the wardrobe. The bat stops glowing and everything goes dark again. I'm really tired now. I climb back into bed and pull my doona over my head. Maybe when I wake up in the morning it will have been a dream. Maybe the Fent will be gone and everything will be back to normal. I sure hope so. I don't know what I'm going to do otherwise.

CHAPTER 3

BREAKFAST TIME

'Curly!' Mum's voice calls from the kitchen. 'Breakfast is ready.'

I roll over and see sunlight streaming through my bedroom window. I feel as though I've only just gone to sleep. Was the Fent a dream, I wonder. I climb out of bed and stand in front of my wardrobe. Should I open the door?

'You'd better get dressed, Curly,' Mum calls again.

My school uniform is inside the wardrobe. I don't have any choice. Taking a deep breath, I jerk the door outwards and jump back. But all I see are clothes and shoes and other junk.

I move closer. 'Fent?' I whisper.

'Are you there?'

There's no reply.

'Hurry up, Curly!' Mum yells. 'I have to call in at your Uncle Jeffrey's on the way to school. We've got to get going!'

I race out to the kitchen – I can deal with the Fent and my uniform in a minute. A bowl of cereal is waiting for me on the table. Mum is standing at the bench, cutting herself up some fruit.

'Morning, Curly!'

'Morning, Mum.'

'Still in your pyjamas? Is that monster still living in your wardrobe?'

I open my mouth, then close it again. 'No, Mum,' I reassure her.

'Glad to hear it.'

For some reason I find myself asking, 'Say if there was a monster – a small monster with pointy ears, who was lost and had nowhere else to go – could he stay with us?'

Mum smiles smugly. 'If it means you won't be waking me up in the middle of the night, then yes, it can stay.'

Boy, talk about rubbing it in.

I'm halfway through my cereal when I hear a chirping noise. The Fent is standing on the bench near Mum.

I choke. Mum turns around.

'Are you okay?'

I nod. Why can't she see him?

'Only kids can see me,' the Fent explains. 'She can't hear me either. And she can't hear you talking to me.'

'Oh.'

He jumps from the bench to the table. 'Your Mum is bigger than you, but she isn't brown.'

I look at Mum, trying to see her how the Fent does. Tall, with long red hair, a grey suit, pale skin. *Not brown.* 'I take after Dad,' I whisper to him. 'He's Aboriginal. Mum's family is from Ireland.'

The Fent looks confused.

I sigh. 'Dad has brown skin, Mum doesn't, and I look like him. Okay?'

'I like brown. I'm brown. I'm going to live with you, Curly. Your mum said so.'

Is that why I asked Mum that question?

Did the Fent make me? I glare at him.

'I like your Mum. I'm going to wear her hat.'

My red underpants suddenly appear on his head. Two feathery ears are poking out through the leg holes.

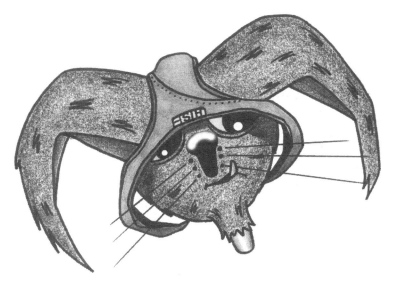

'Take them off!'

The Fent looks unhappy. He pulls a face, then whips my underpants off his head and flings them into the air. They land on top of Mum's freshly cut bowl of fruit.

'Curly!' she says angrily. 'That's not funny!'

She grabs the undies and storms off to the laundry to throw them in the washing machine.

'Hehehe,' the Fent chuckles.

'Stop getting me in trouble,' I growl.

He sticks his tongue out at me and vanishes.

Mum comes back into the room. She looks at the bench. 'Where's my fruit?'

I look too. The bowl is empty.

'It wasn't me, Mum . . .' I say, ready to dob in the Fent. 'It was the one-eyed beast. The Fent. Only really he's got two eyes.'

'Don't, Curly!' She shakes her head. 'If you want fruit, you can have fruit. Fruit is good for you. Just stop blaming everything on your imaginary friend, okay?'

I'm angry now. Really angry. That fat, greedy, lying Fent is nothing but trouble!

CHAPTER 4

GOING TO SCHOOL

As I climb into the car to go to school, the Fent appears next to me in the back seat. I look out the window to see Billy Green, an older kid who lives next door to us, walk by the fence. He's dressed to go to school too. The same school as me, unfortunately. He sees me looking at him and pulls a face, and then his mouth hangs open in astonishment. Uh oh. He's seen the Fent. The Fent gives Billy a little wave.

'Don't!' I whisper, as the Fent grins at me.
Fortunately, Mum starts reversing the car
and we pull out into the street, away from
Billy. The Fent is annoying, but I wouldn't
want someone like Billy getting a hold of
him.

'Where are we going, Curly?' asks the
Fent.

'School. You can't come.'

'I am,' he replies with a sneaky look. 'I am coming.'

'No you're not.'

'If I make you laugh, can I come?'

'You can't make me laugh.'

'Why not?'

'Because I'm angry with you.'

He pulls a feather off his leg. Then he darts over, sticks the feather under my arm and tickles me. I try to push him away.

'Sit still, Curly,' Mum complains. 'Don't

bump the back of the seat while I'm driving.'

I want to sit still, but I can't. He's found my most ticklish spot. I keep my teeth clenched to stop myself from laughing and try to grab him, but he slips out of my hands. I lunge towards him, only to be jerked back by my seatbelt.

'Curly!' Mum yells.

'I'm sorry, Mum! It was an accident.'

The Fent clings to the top of the front passenger seat and teases me by wiggling the feather.

When we arrive at Uncle Jeffrey's house the Fent loses interest in me. He stands on the seat and presses his face against the glass of the window, watching as Mum goes into the house.

'Ooh. Red,' he says, staring at Uncle Jeffrey's brand new Toyota. 'I like red.'

'That's Uncle Jeffrey's,' I tell him. '*No one's* allowed to touch it. Not even me.'

Actually, *especially* not me – Uncle

Jeffrey still hasn't forgiven me for spilling a milkshake in his last car. I eye the Fent nervously. If he does something to the car, I know I'll get the blame. Luckily, Mum soon comes out carrying some papers, and I sigh with relief. Only a few blocks to school now.

As we get back on the road, the Fent jumps on top of my head and brushes his feather over my face.

Time to get my revenge!

'Argh!' I shout, flinging my hands up. 'My eye! I can't see!'

Mum glances in her rear-vision mirror and sees me pretend to cry. 'Are you okay, Curly? What did you do?'

The Fent is looking upset.

I take my hands off my face and grin. 'Tricked you!'

Mum catches me smiling. 'CURLY! Don't play silly games like that! It's not funny!'

'Sorry, Mum!'

I smirk at the Fent and whisper, 'Gotcha!'

The Fent sniffs. 'Your mum is right. That's not funny!'

'Sore loser.'

He presses himself back into the corner and looks out the window. He is still sulking when we pull up outside the school. I jump out, but the Fent stays put.

Mum calls after me. 'Your dad is picking you up today.'

Oh great. Now everyone will see his crazy car again.

'Have a good day, Curly – and be good!'

As the car pulls away, I see the Fent's face pressed against the rear window. It feels good to get away from him. I'd rather the Fent spend the day with Mum than cause me problems at school.

CHAPTER 5

POISON FRUIT

'Curly . . .' someone calls softly. My friend Chris is signalling me from behind the library wall. I go over to him. His hair is ruffled and his clothes are all messed up.

'Was it Billy?' I ask.

He nods. 'He took my lunch money. He says if I want it back, you have to ask for it.'

'Me?' I squeak in surprise.

'What have you done, Curly?'

'Nothing.'

'Can you get my lunch money back?'

'I don't know. Look, you can share my lunch today. Okay?'

He nods in agreement.

The bell goes and we walk towards our class. There is a sinking feeling in my stomach. I know what Billy really wants. He wants the Fent.

I find it hard to concentrate. Mr Andrews keeps yelling at me for not paying attention. He's not the most popular teacher in the school. He gets upset over little things. Over everything, really. He writes long letters to students' parents telling them how bad they are at schoolwork, and he never forgets anything. At the end of the year he can still tell you what you did wrong during the first week of school.

Towards lunchtime, Mr Andrews announces that he has a surprise for us. No one looks happy. None of his surprises are ever any fun.

'A surprise *test*!' he chuckles gleefully.

We all groan.

'Be prepared for the unexpected,' he tells us as he hands out the test. 'That is the most important lesson to learn in life.'

'This is *so* unfair!' I mutter to Chris.

I forgot Mr Andrews has superhuman hearing. He turns on me like a short, bald shark.

'Unfair? Life is unfair, Mr Curly. You had better get used to it. For speaking without putting your hand up, I am deducting ten marks from your test.'

I open my mouth to protest.

'Something else to say, Mr Curly?'

What's the point? He'll just take off more marks. I close my mouth again.

'Good, at least you've learnt something today. All right class, you have thirty minutes to complete the test. Starting . . . now!'

I stare at the paper. I can't answer the first question, or the second, and I don't even understand what the third one is about. So I just sit there. *Who cares about a stupid test, anyway?* I have a bigger problem to solve. Picking up my pen I draw a picture of Billy's face next to question four. Then I hear a small voice whisper, 'This is boring, Curly.'

The Fent is lounging on the floor near my desk. For some reason no one else seems to notice him. I wonder why not?

'Go away!' I hiss.

He ignores me and begins rolling around
in small circles on the floor, like it's some
kind of game. He bumps my desk and it
moves.

'What is that noise?' Mr Andrews
demands.

I hunch lower in my seat, but he's already
looking at me.

'Mr Curly. Again. Your desk has
mysteriously moved, I see. Are you trying to
cheat?'

He comes over and picks up my paper.
'You haven't written anything, Mr Curly!
Perhaps you *need* to cheat.'

Everyone giggles. Then Mr Andrews turns
the page over and sees Billy's face glaring at
him from question four.

'Pictures, Mr Curly? I think you'd better
sit down the front with me.'

There is a spare desk next to his own

where he puts the students he wants to pick on.

I gather up my paper and pen and go to the front of the class. The Fent follows me.

'My stomach is making horrible noises,' he moans. 'I don't think Fents should eat fruit.' He rolls on the floor near my new desk, clutching his middle.

I hope fruit isn't poisonous to Fents.

Mr Mason, the Headmaster, suddenly sticks his head around the door.

'A nice, quiet class,' he says, smiling. 'With all the students working hard.'

He sees me sitting at the front and frowns. 'I just want a quiet word with Mr Andrews, everyone. Carry on with your work. Especially you, Curly.'

Mr Andrews goes to the door and he and Mason begin discussing something. I just hope it's not me. I start reading question five.

'Pushing the poison out,' the Fent declares, red-faced.

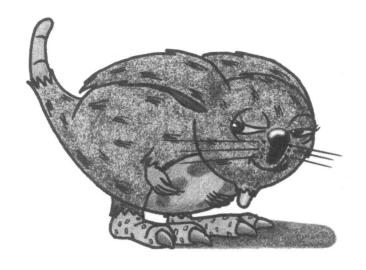

There is a loud farting sound. Muffled giggles spread across the room.

'Curly!' Mr Andrews snaps in disgust. 'You will apologise to Mr Mason and the rest of the class this instant.'

'But it wasn't me!'

The Fent rolls across the floor to Mr Andrews' legs and lets out a real beauty. It stinks too; I can smell it all the way from here. The whole class is shocked. Mr Mason steps away. He pinches his nose, trying not to breathe.

'It wasn't me!' Mr Andrews mutters under his breath. His face is bright red.

'Be prepared for the unexpected!' Chris calls out from the back of the class. Everyone bursts out laughing. Mr Mason calls the class to order, but all the kids are making farting noises with their mouths. He tells us to put our pens down and sends us out for an early lunch.

'Hehehe,' the Fent chuckles smugly.

'You are *never* eating fruit again!' I tell him.

CHAPTER 6

BILLY

I am sharing my lunch with Chris when I see Billy on the other side of the playground. He's looking in my direction. He signals to me. Suddenly I don't feel hungry any more. Billy goes to sit on a big rock at the edge of the bush that fringes the grass. He thinks he's the king of the school when he sits there. Luckily he hasn't spotted the Fent yet.

'Listen,' I tell the Fent. 'I need you to

disappear for a while. There's a kid I have to speak to and I'm afraid he can see you.'

'Only you can see me now,' he replies. 'That's how I made it.'

So that's why no one else saw him in class.

'I don't want to take any chances! Just go, will you?'

The Fent frowns, then vanishes.

By the time I reach Billy my knees feel sweaty and weak with fear. Billy smiles his mean little smile, but doesn't say anything.

He just lets me stand in front of him and wait. I start counting all the ways he can hurt me, and sweat even more. Finally he speaks. 'So, Curly. What was that weird thing I saw in your car this morning?'

I think for a moment, then reply. 'You mean my mum?'

I'm really glad she's not here to hear me say that.

'Very funny, Curly. I mean that ugly, hairy thing with the pointy ears that was sitting in the back with you.'

'Oh. Our new dog.'

'Dog?'

'Dad bought it for me from overseas.'

Billy had met my dad, so it wouldn't be hard for him to believe he'd bought me a weird dog. Dad buys a lot of weird things.

'It didn't look like a dog to me.'

'That's because it's from somewhere else. They have a lot of different dogs in other countries.'

'Is it a hunting dog?'

Billy reckons his dog is a hunting dog. I think it's just been driven crazy from living with Billy and his dad.

'My dog's just a pet. He's not like Killer.'

Amazingly, Billy doesn't look angry. I decide to push my luck. 'Can I have Chris's money now?'

To my surprise he pulls Chris's five-dollar note out of his pocket. But when I go to take it, he grabs my hand and twists it until it hurts. 'I want to meet that dog, Curly. *Tomorrow.*'

He lets my hand go. It's red and it feels sore where his fingers dug in.

Billy grins at me. 'You can go now, Curly. Run back to your little friend Chris and tell him he's never getting his money back. I'll see you tomorrow.'

I turn and walk away very quickly. Tomorrow is Saturday; it will be hard to dodge him. What am I going to do?

CHAPTER 7

THE MAD INVENTOR

When school is over, I wait out the front for Dad. Maybe he'll be late. If he's late then no one will see the car. I haven't seen it for a week myself. In a week, anything could have happened to it. It could've changed shape and colour, grown wings or gained giant wheels. Dad is an inventor, so he's always experimenting on it. He believes in looking after the earth too, so it runs on fuel made out of potato skins.

The fuel stinks worse than the Fent's farts. Uncle Jeffrey thinks Dad is crazy. I love my dad, but when it comes to some of his inventions, I think he's a little crazy too.

I see the smoke first. Dad will be unhappy with that; it's not good for the air. Then I hear the noise. He'll be unhappy with that, too. Noise pollution. And finally, there's the smell. I put my hand over my mouth

and nose and watch as a rainbow-coloured Holden sedan with a solar panel tied to the roof chugs slowly around the corner. From the front seat a brown-skinned, curly-haired man waves madly at me.

'Jump in, son!' Dad shouts as he draws closer, surrounded by a cloud of purple smoke. He never stops the car unless he has to, because it usually doesn't start again.

The front side door springs open as the car crawls past, and I run a few steps and leap inside. Around me all the other kids are coughing and laughing.

'Woohoo!' Dad yells. 'Great run, Curly! You'll make the Olympics yet.'

Dad is enthusiastic about everything I do.

'I thought you were buying a new car,' I grumble.

'I was, but then I had a new idea instead. Better to spend your money on a new idea than a new car. You buy a new car one day, and the next day it's worth half what you paid for it. Only idiots buy new cars.'

He means Uncle Jeffrey. They don't get on.

I sigh. 'So, what's your new idea?'

'Edible soap!' he replies excitedly.

'What?!'

'Our rivers are very polluted with all the detergents that flow into them, Curly, and it's bad for the river animals. But my soap's suds will feed the fish and frogs in the rivers, and humans can eat the soap too!'

I try to imagine washing my bum and then eating the leftover soap.

'I don't think people will want to eat food they've just cleaned themselves with, Dad.'

He looks thoughtful. 'Good point, son, good point. But every brilliant idea has its drawbacks. It might all be in the marketing. And you know what I've always told you – when I make my first million, I'll buy you a truckload of toys. A whole truckload, Curly!'

He sounds more excited about it than I am.

'It might take a long time to make edible soap, Dad. It might cost a lot of money.'

His Super Sunscreen had cost a lot of money. You were supposed to be able to put it on once, and it would last forever. Lucky for me it didn't, or I'd still be bright orange.

'You're thinking about the sunscreen, aren't you?' Dad asks.

I nod. It's scary how he sometimes knows exactly what's on my mind.

'This idea is different, Curly.'

They always were.

'This idea will *work*.'

They never did.

'And it *won't* take a long time, because I've already got a batch made up! I want you to be the first to try it!'

'Have you ever heard of a Fent, Dad?' I ask, trying to change the subject.

'The world is a wonderful place, Curly,' he says with a twinkle in his eye. 'There are a lot of things I haven't heard of, but that doesn't mean they don't exist. '

'It's like a small animal with pointy ears and big feet. There's one living in my wardrobe.'

'Really? I had a mouse living in my wardrobe once.'

'This isn't the same, Dad.'

'Well, I hope you're looking after it, Curly!

I looked after the mouse. I named him Thomas and fed him cheese.'

I sigh and give up.

We pull up at the front of our house. Uncle Jeffrey's red Toyota is parked in the drive. Mum comes out straight away. 'Hello, Martin. Curly, can you go inside and say hello to your Uncle Jeffrey? Your father and I will be in shortly.'

She always sends me inside when she wants to talk to Dad about something she doesn't want me to hear.

'See you later, Dad.'

'In a minute, son.'

Uncle Jeffrey is sitting on the couch, looking large and red-haired and awkward. He's Mum's brother, and he has no idea how to talk to kids.

'Afternoon, Curly,' he says as I walk in.

'Hello, Uncle Jeffrey.'

'Did you have a good day at school?'

'Yes. Did you have a good day at work?'

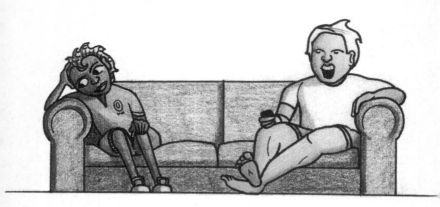

'Yes.'

We both sit there. After a while he gets up and sneaks a look out the window.
I look too.

'Don't spy on your parents!' Uncle Jeffrey growls.

I sit back down.

He keeps on spying.

Finally Mum and Dad walk up to the front porch. Uncle Jeffrey dives back onto the couch and flicks on the TV with the remote.
I hear Mum and Dad talking.

'He's just got a great imagination,' Dad says.

'Yes, and I know where he gets it from!'

They come inside. Dad leans down and shakes hands with Uncle Jeffrey.

'Jeff.'

'Martin.'

Dad glances at the TV. 'Didn't know you were a fan of the Wiggles, Jeff.'

'I'm not watching it! Curly is.'

Dad winks at me. He knows I'm way too old for the Wiggles.

'Come and say goodbye, Curly.'

We go outside and say goodbye the way we always do – by pushing the car down the street until it starts. Dad jumps in as it begins to take off.

'Say hello to the Fent for me!' he calls.

Then a small package comes flying through the air and hits me in the chest.

'Have a taste, Curly.' Dad orders as he rolls away. 'Edible soap is going to be the biggest thing since Coca-Cola!'

When I go back inside, Mum and Uncle

Jeffrey are whispering to each other in the kitchen. Mum seems to be trying to persuade him to do something that he obviously doesn't want to do. Finally, they come back into the lounge and Uncle Jeffrey says, 'Um – would you like to go for a ride in *my* car, Curly?'

Wow. This is Mum's doing. Ever since the milkshake incident I've been banned.

'Thanks, Uncle Jeffrey.'

But when we go out the front, his car isn't in the driveway any more. It's across the other side of the road with its rear end backed into a light pole. We all rush over. Uncle Jeffrey circles it in disbelief. 'This will cost thousands of dollars to fix,' he mutters to himself. 'Thousands.'

He looks like he's going to cry.

I peer inside. The handbrake is off.

'Hehehe,' I hear a small voice say. 'I *like* red cars.'

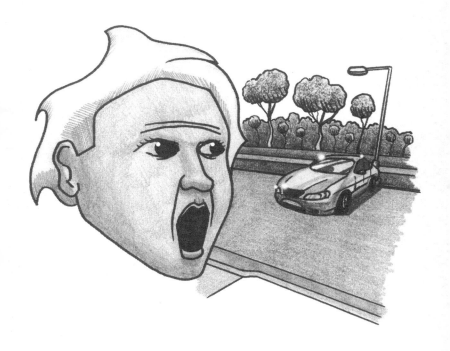

CHAPTER 8

BILLY COMES HUNTING

When we're alone I growl at the Fent. I'm worried he might try to drive Mum's car, and she can't afford to get it fixed. He retreats inside the wardrobe. I pull out the little plastic bag Dad threw at me and peer inside. The soap is brown and mushy and it looks like dog poo. I put a tiny bit on my tongue. EWWW!

The Fent appears on my bed. 'I want some!'

He grabs the bag and swallows the lot.

'Hmm, yummy.'

Suddenly his eyes roll up and he flops back, groaning. Has Dad's soap killed him? I put my hand on his chest, trying to see if he's breathing. His eyes fly open.

'More!'

'More?'

'Better than fruit!'

I laugh. Maybe there's a use for Dad's soap after all.

When I wake up the next morning it's Saturday. Luckily for me, the Fent is nowhere to be seen. Maybe he's gone for the day. I hope so. If he's not here, then Billy can't hurt him. I check the wardrobe to make sure he's not hiding under my clothes. Ugh! My wardrobe smells of the Fent. But he's nowhere to be seen. Mum comes into my room. 'Want some breakfast, Curly?'

'No thanks, Mum! I'm going to the park.'

The park is across the road. I figure I can keep a watch for Billy from there and for the Fent too. I plan to tell Billy my new dog is with Dad. It's the best story I can think of.

'Don't wander too far, Curly,' Mum says. 'I'm going to work on my tax return. Maybe we'll get some money back, eh?'

Mum's always short of money.

'Dad's new idea might work out, Mum,' I reassure her. 'You never know.'

She just shakes her head.

'Dad tries his best, Mum, he's just – well, he's Dad.'

'I know Curly,' she says. 'He's a good man at heart. He's just not very . . . practical.'

Then she notices my fallen expression.

'He tries to do the right thing.' She smiles reassuringly at me.

'That's important, isn't it, Mum? Even if it gets you into trouble.'

She nods. I'm thinking of all the crazy

things I might have to do to protect the Fent. When I open my wardrobe door again, I wonder if I should bother. All my clean clothes smell of Fent. I spot my school uniform on the floor, where I flung it yesterday. Maybe no one will notice? I sigh and put it on.

I haven't been at the park very long when some other kids turn up. It's never empty on a Saturday. They laugh at my clothes for a few seconds, but everyone's more interested in getting on with a game of football. I'm really having fun until Billy comes storming across the road.

'Hey Curly!' he shouts angrily, then he pauses for a second. 'Nice uniform, loser. 'I just saw your dad down the shops and you don't have a new dog!'

Uh oh. As if today wasn't going badly enough. All the kids look at each other. There's one thing you can say about Billy – he's fair. When he's mad, he doesn't care who he bashes. Everyone takes off.

'I'm gonna get you, Curly!' Billy shouts. 'I'm gonna hunt you down with Killer!'

I panic. Billy is between me and my house, so I turn and run in the other direction, heading for the bushland by the river. I've hidden there from Billy before, maybe I can again.

The Fent appears as I'm racing through the paperbark trees. I don't stop. I haven't got much of a head start and I need to

make the most of it.

'Where are we going, Curly?' he asks.

'I'm going to hide so Billy can't find me,' I pant hoarsely. 'And you're going to disappear!'

'Again?'

'Again!'

'Booorrring! Is hiding boring, too?'

'Yes!'

He points to the sky. 'What's that, Curly?'

'A pelican. Now *go away*!'

He bounds off in another direction. I don't have time to follow him so I keep running. The bush starts to grows thicker and the light thinner. The ground beneath my feet feels soft and muddy – I must be getting near the water. Sure enough, I come out of the scrub at the edge of the river. There are pelicans everywhere.

'I'm hiding!' a small voice chirps. 'Can you see me, Curly?'

'This is no time for games!' I yell. I look

around but I can't see the Fent. Then I spot two fluffy ears sticking out of the beak of a nearby pelican.

'Get out of there!' I shout.

The Fent climbs out and grins at me. 'Not boring!' he says.

He starts rolling around in the shallows. I try to catch him, but he's too slippery.

'Curr-lyy!' Billy's voice rings through the bush. 'Cuuurr-lyyy!'

I can hear Killer snarling.

The Fent looks frightened. 'His dog can smell me,' he sighs.

'He can probably smell me, too.'

Maybe this isn't such a great hiding place after all.

'You have to go!' I tell the Fent.

'I don't want to leave you!'

I grab him and take off like a frightened rabbit.

Billy calls again. 'Why don't you come out, Curly? I just want to play with your pet.'

I know what kind of games Billy likes to play. He likes to break things. I won't let him break the Fent.

'They'll be on us soon.' I hiss. 'Disappear *now*!'

The Fent hangs his head. 'I just tried, Curly. I can't do it. My magic's been funny ever since I ate the yummy soap.'

I should've guessed. Dad's inventions always have unexpected side effects.

'Does that mean Billy can see you again?'

He nods. I run faster, crashing through some spiky bushes that scratch my arms and legs. It hurts, but I don't let the Fent go. There is a fallen log up ahead – maybe I can hide there. I leap over it, only to land with a muddy splash. *The swamp!* My feet sink into the ground. I try to move but my foot is tangled in some thick reeds in the water. Behind me, I hear Billy let out a triumphant howl. He's seen us! So has Killer.

I throw the Fent forward.

'Run!' I yell.

Something big and black flies past me. Killer. He grabs the Fent in his jaws, and I hear a scream. Killer snarls at me and bounds back to Billy. I twist my head to see him drop the Fent at Billy's feet.

'Fent!' I shout. But he just lies there, all limp and still.

Billy picks him up by the ears and shoves him in his backpack. 'You should have shared him with me, Curly. Now you'll be stuck here while I'm playing games with your rat.' He laughs nastily and walks away, leaving me alone in the swamp.

I go to work trying to free myself. Nothing is going to stop me from doing what I have to do. I've got a friend to save. Sure he gets me into trouble a lot, but he's my mate. *Please don't let him be dead*, I think as I twist my foot in the reeds, trying to get it loose. I finally manage to wriggle out of my shoe and limp home. I'm muddy, exhausted and sick with worry.

But when I get there, I find my luck isn't all bad. Billy is out the front of his house mowing the lawn. His dad is on the verandah shouting at him. 'When you've finished that, Billy, you can start on the pruning. If you'd been here when you promised, then you would've been finished by now.'

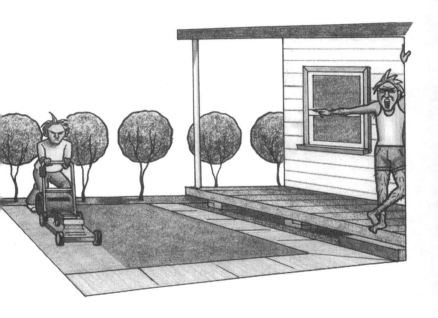

Saturday is Billy's chore day. He must have skipped out on his dad to chase me. This is great. He hasn't had time to torment the Fent. I have a chance to save him. If he's still alive.

CHAPTER 9

CURLY GOES HUNTING

I spend the rest of the day spying on Billy's house. I know the Fent will be in the rickety shed in the backyard. That's where Billy hides everything he steals. But with Killer roaming around, I can't get in there. I have to wait until night-time when Killer's chained up. Luckily, Billy's dad is still mad at him. He keeps finding new gardening jobs for him to do. If he'd been any other dad, I guess I could just pretend the Fent really is a dog or something, and go ask for him back. But there is something about Billy's dad that's even scarier than Billy. The afternoon drags on for what seems like forever, but it finally starts to get dark. Killer is chained up, and Billy and his dad are inside their house. I tell Mum I don't feel well enough to eat dinner and I'm going to have an early night. She thinks that's a good idea. Once I'm in my bedroom I shut the door, then climb out my window and sneak towards the loose pickets in our side fence.

I squeeze through and look around Billy's yard cautiously. Far to my right, there is a stake in the ground with a chain attached. The chain disappears into a big kennel. Killer must be asleep. To my left is the shed, leaning against the back fence. I creep towards it. I'm almost there when I step on a stick. It only makes a small sound, but it's enough to alert Killer. He rushes out snarling, and I fling open the door and

sprint into the shed.

'Fent! Fent, where are you?'
I ask urgently.

There's no reply. Maybe he isn't here after all. I peer into the darkness.

'Fent, it's me, Curly. I've come to rescue you.'

Still nothing. I feel like crying. Is the Fent gone? Is he dead? Outside, the dog snarls louder, snapping and choking on the end of its chain. I probably don't have much longer until Billy or his dad comes to investigate.

'Fent!' I plead, one last time.

A small voice whispers, 'Curly?'

Diving in the direction of the sound, I find Billy's backpack and rip it open. The Fent leaps out. 'You came!' he cries. 'Are you going to slay the evil monster?'

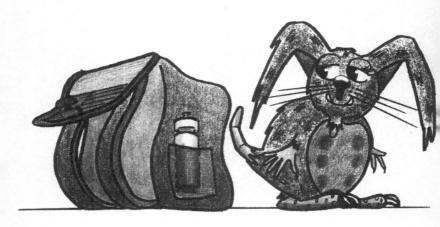

'I think we'd better just get out of here.'
But then I hear the back door open.
'I know that's you, Curly!' Billy shouts. 'You can't have him. He's mine!'
I dive out of the shed, and Billy speeds across the yard towards me. I race for the fence but Killer leaps in front of it.

That chain is longer than I thought! I dodge both of them and veer back towards Billy's house.

'Run fast, Curly!' the Fent urges. 'Or the hunters will catch you.'

Then he pokes his head up over my shoulder and blows a fart noise.

'Don't do that!' I yell. 'You'll make them even madder!'

I lurch into Billy's house and slam the door shut behind me. I hear the lock click shut. Billy starts banging on the door with his fist. His dad calls out, 'Billy? Is that you?'

Panicking, I dash down the hall and dive inside the first room I see. I shut the door and press my ear against it, trying to listen to what's going on. Footsteps go past me, and Billy's dad speaks again. 'What are you doing?'

The back door creaks open, and I hear Billy say, 'Sorry, Dad. The door closed behind me and I locked myself out.'

'That's no reason to attack the door! Come and help me with the dinner dishes!'

Billy and his dad walk past the room where I'm hiding, towards the front of the house. The Fent tugs at my arm but I push him away. 'Not now, Fent!'

I keep my ear to the door for another few minutes, but I don't hear anything else. Maybe we can escape after all.

The Fent tugs my arm again. 'Look, Curly. Scary.'

I turn around to growl at him, but then I see what he's been looking at. Scattered on the floor are horrible pictures of Fents. They are drawn with red eyes, sharp claws and big teeth. They look like monsters.

'I found them in the desk,' the Fent says in a small voice.

I look around. This must be Mr Green's study. There is a computer on the desk. Next to it is a strange metal object that looks like some kind of a homemade gun.

I shiver. I have to get the Fent out of here.
I go over to the window and open it, but
before I can leave the door opens behind
me.

'Got you!' Billy crows triumphantly.

The Fent bounces up right in front of him
and wiggles his little hand.

Billy freezes. Then his face crumbles, and he starts blubbering like a baby. 'I'm sorry! I'm so sorry!'

'My magic's back,' the Fent tells me triumphantly.

'What did you do?'

'I made him feel what I felt when he was mean to me,' he says smugly.

Heavy footsteps are approaching down the hall. I grab the Fent. 'We have to go!'

We dive out the window, landing in the bushes. I can hear Billy's dad shouting from inside. 'What are you doing in here, Billy? Why are my pictures on the floor? I told you never to go into my desk!'

I press myself onto the ground under the bushes, cradling the Fent against me. I don't want Billy's dad to look out and see us.

Billy is still crying. 'I'm sorry, Dad! I'll never hurt Curly's Fent again! I promise!'

'FENT?! Where did you hear that word? Have you seen one?'

'I caught one, but it's gone.'

Billy's dad growls loudly, 'Disappeared, has it? That's what they do, Billy. One minute they're here, the next they're gone. And no one believes you. They just think you're crazy. My mum and dad never believed me. But don't worry, lad. If Curly's got one, then we'll hunt it down.'

'But I don't want to hunt it any more!'

'Don't be stupid. Of course you do. We'll catch that monster together! I've been after one for years.'

I jump to my feet and make a run for it with the Fent pressed to my chest. Hiding in the next lot of bushes, I check to make sure Billy's dad hasn't seen us. Then I dart across my front yard and around the side of my house to my bedroom. We climb back in through the window, and I crash onto my bed. My legs just won't hold me up any more. The Fent bounces on the floor, then rolls around happily.

'Thank you for saving me, Curly.
Thank you, thank you, thank you!'

He darts inside my wardrobe. I guess he
feels safe in there. 'Are we friends, Curly?'
he calls out.

'Yeah, Fent. We're friends.'

There is a pause, then Fent says,
'Goodnight, Curly!'

'Night, Fent.'

Just as I'm dozing off he speaks again.
'Billy's dad is very mean, Curly.'

'I know.'

When I fall asleep, I dream about the
awful gun.

CHAPTER 10

CAPTURED!

The Fent and I spend Sunday hiding – him in the wardrobe, me in my room. He's got big bruises and some bad scratches under his feathers from where Killer grabbed him and shook him.

Billy's dad sits out on the verandah staring at our house. I don't know what to do. I wish I knew how to send the Fent home. His parents must be missing him by now. I wonder if they're looking for him.

Do they even have any idea where he is?
At least his magic is back, so he can protect
himself by disappearing. I can't disappear
though. Maybe I should be hiding in the
wardrobe with him.

The next morning I tell the Fent to stay
vanished until I get home from school.
When Mum and I leave the house, Billy's
dad is still sitting on the verandah. I wonder
if he's been there all night. Mum gives him
a friendly wave.

Don't, Mum, I think. *Just don't.* I don't want him coming over and talking to us.

We climb into the car and she puts the key in the ignition, but the car won't start. Mum turns the key again and again, but nothing happens. Billy's dad strolls over. He smiles at Mum.

'Engine giving you trouble, Jane? I can drive Curly to school, if you like. I was just about to take Billy.'

Oh great!

Mum looks relieved. 'Thanks, Ian. I've got a busy day at the office, I really need to get going.'

'You could call a taxi. I'll wait until it comes, if you like. If you can't get one I'll drop you at work too.' He smiles again.

I can't believe Mum is agreeing to this. Can't she see how fake he is?

When Mum goes inside to call a taxi, I follow her.

'Mum, you can't leave me with him.'

Mum looks at me. 'Why, what is it?'

'He wants the Fent!'

Mum groans. 'Curly, I really don't have time for this today. Mr Green is a perfectly nice man, and trust me, he has no interest in your imaginary friend.'

I try to explain, but of course she doesn't believe me. In no time at all she is speeding away in a taxi, leaving me alone with Billy's dad. His hand falls heavily on my shoulder. 'Let's go to my house, Curly. Billy is waiting for us there.'

I try to get away but he's really strong.

'Come on, Curly. We're going to have a nice long talk. Just the three of us.'

Mr Green drags me inside and hustles me down the hall into the horrible study. Billy is already in there, sitting on the floor with his back pressed to the wall. He doesn't look happy. Mr Green locks the door behind us.

'Is it here, Billy?' he asks. 'Has Curly brought the Fent with him?'

Billy shakes his head miserably. I almost feel sorry for him.

'Right then,' says Mr Green. 'We'll just wait. I've waited this long to see a Fent again. I can wait a little bit longer. You tell me the moment you see it, Billy!'

He goes and sits behind his desk. There is a big cage on top of it. I guess it's for the Fent. I imagine him trapped in there and feel sick.

Mr Green opens a drawer and pulls out his strange gun. 'You see this, Curly? This is for Fents. I've spent years designing it.' He looks at his invention fondly. 'Everyone said I was crazy, Curly. But now I'm going to show them. I'm going to prove to the world that Fents are real.' He smiles at me, but there's nothing reassuring about it. 'You look upset, Curly. Why don't you go sit with Billy? I don't want to hurt you. I just want the Fent.'

I sit down next to Billy. Mr Green leans back in his chair and points his gun into the air around the room. His blue eyes are glittering and his face is flushed.

'I'm sorry, Curly,' Billy whispers. 'I really am.'

'I know,' I whisper back. 'Don't worry. We'll find a way out of this.'

Funnily enough, that seems to make him feel better. Who would ever have thought Billy would be relying on me?

I try to think of what to do. I don't want to call the Fent in case that gun really can hurt him. I have to come up with something else. Then I think of my dad, about the way he sometimes knows exactly what's in my head. He told me once that it was because we had a special connection. 'If you're ever in trouble, Curly, I mean *really* in trouble, you just think of me. You call for help, and I'll come.' Okay, it was right after he and Mum had split up, and maybe he was just trying to make me feel better. But who knows, it might work. I was really in trouble now, and it wasn't as if I had anything else to try. I close my eyes and concentrate harder than I ever have before. *Dad*, I shout in my mind. *Help, Dad! Mr Green's got me locked in his study!*

I have no way of knowing if it worked or not. I just have to wait. Billy and I sit there in the corner for what seems like hours. Mr Green keeps muttering about Fents. I hear some cars come down the street and stop close by. Doors slam. Feet come pounding towards the house. Billy and I look at each other. Mr Green is polishing his gun with a faraway look in his eyes. Soon there is hammering at the front door.

'Let me in!' Dad shouts through the door. 'I know you have my son in there!'

Mr Green jumps up, looking furious. I don't want him to fight my dad. Billy leaps to his feet and points to the window, yelling 'FENT!'

I almost stop breathing, until I realise

there's nothing there. Billy is trying to trick him. Mr Green rushes over to the window with his gun. Billy and I leap onto his back and he stumbles and falls to the floor. The gun rolls away. Dad, Mum and Uncle Jeffrey appear at the window and look in.

'Hold on, son!' Dad yells. 'I'm coming!'

'We're all coming!' says Uncle Jeffrey, as he gives me the thumbs-up sign.

I wonder how they are going to get in. Mr Green is getting up. Billy and I dive for the gun together.

Uncle Jeffrey levers the window open and they all climb in. Dad and Uncle Jeffrey grab Mr Green. Mum helps me and Billy to our feet. 'Are you boys all right?' she cries. There are tears in her eyes.

'We're okay, Mum.'

We hand her the gun.

'Dad was going to use it on the Fent,' Billy says sheepishly.

She looks at him as if she's thinking, *Oh no, not another one.*

Dad and Uncle Jeffrey have made Mr Green sit down and they are talking to him. He is threatening to sue them for breaking and entering.

'We knew you were in trouble, Curly,' she adds. 'A little voice kept whispering to all of us, "Curly is in trouble. Curly is in trouble." It must have been our intuition.'

I shake my head. Mum still hasn't put two and two together. How could the three of them all have heard a mysterious voice in their heads at the same time? Right on cue, the Fent appears in the middle of the room.

'Curly! I sent your family! I used all my magic! I *saved* you!'

Billy and I grin at each other.

'Thanks,' I say.

CHAPTER 11

FAREWELL TO THE FENT

The Fent is really proud of himself. He can't stop boasting. 'It was *hard*, Curly. I had to use every bit of my magic. Am I a hero?'

'Of course you are!' I tell him.

Before I can say more there is a bright flash of light. I blink. The room is filled with Fents. Big Fents. *Really* big Fents.

The Fent squeals in delight. 'Mum, Dad, Grandma, Grandpa, Uncle Kip, Aunty Soo . . .'

He goes on and on. His whole family must be here.

The biggest one of all is as tall as Mum – but a lot wider. It picks the Fent up and speaks sternly, 'We've been looking for you everywhere, Pook! What are you doing in this strange "Earth" world? If you hadn't used so much magic at once we might never have found you!'

Pook, I think. *Pook? The Fent has a name?*

Mr Green is watching Billy's face.
'It's here, isn't it, Billy?'

He bursts away from Dad and Uncle Jeffrey and grabs the gun from Mum.

'Where is it? *Where is it?*' He waves his horrible invention in the air. We all throw ourselves on the floor. From underneath my arm I see a laser beam from the gun hit the Fents.

But it doesn't hurt them at all.

Then Mum gasps. So does Uncle Jeffrey. Dad just grins as though he's made the best discovery in the whole world. The adults can see the Fents! So *that's* what the gun was for!

'See?' Mr Green shouts. 'See? They're real! They're real!'

We get up off the floor. The big Fent gives Pook to someone else to hold, and walks towards the adults. He picks Mr Green up, gives him a good shake until he drops the gun, then lets him go. Another Fent picks the gun up and crushes it in his hands.

'No!' Mr Green screams. 'That was the only way I could get proof!'

He lurches forward and plucks a feather from the nearest Fent.

'Aha!' he screams. 'A feather! A Fent feather. That's proof enough.'

He darts to the window. Uncle Jeffrey lunges for him, but one of the Fents puts a big hand on his shoulder and shakes his head. Mr Green throws himself through the open window and runs off down the street, cackling madly.

'Don't worry, Billy,' Mum says. 'We'll get your dad back.'

I look at Billy. I'm not sure he wants him back.

'That's my friend Curly!' Pook announces to everyone in the room. 'I've been living in his wardrobe. That's Curly's dad, who makes yummy food. And that's his mum. I don't like her fruit. And that's his Uncle Jeffrey. I had a ride in his car.'

Uncle Jeffrey looks suspicious.

'And that's Billy. He was mean before, but he's nice now.'

Billy hangs his head and stares at the carpet.

'Thank you for looking after Pook,' his

dad says. 'I hope he hasn't been too much trouble. He's very young.'

'Er, no . . . he's been, I mean . . . he's my friend.'

'I have to go home now, Curly,' Pook says sadly. 'Will you miss me?'

I nod, blinking back tears.

He grins. 'Keep your wardrobe door open for me,' he whispers.

There is another flash of light, and they all disappear.

CHAPTER 12

EVERYTHING CHANGES

After Pook left, everything changed. First, Mum decided that from now on she'd believe everything I told her. Uncle Jeffrey didn't think it was a good idea, but Dad had a good laugh about it. Then there was Mr Green. He came back later that night, but he was a different man. I mean, *really* different. His ears were bigger and hairier and his nose was flatter. He was different on the inside, too.

He was kind, and friendly, and fun. In fact, he was less like a human being and more like a Fent. When Billy told me his dad had been playing the rolling game, I wondered whether a Fent feather had other uses besides tickling. Maybe it wasn't such a good idea to steal one.

Billy has changed too. He's not the school bully any more. He's my friend. Actually, Chris and I are the only friends he's got, since no one else believes he's given up bashing other kids. I like having Billy for a mate, and not only because it means he's not beating me up any longer. It's good to have another kid to talk to about the Fents.

Then there's Dad's edible soap. Pook told the Fents all about it, and they asked Dad for a sample. I explained to Dad how it interfered with their magic, so he experimented until he'd fixed the problem. The Fents loved the stuff! Dad offered to

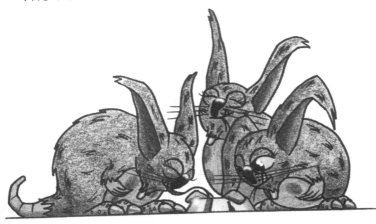

give them the recipe, but they said that wasn't right: Dad had invented it so they couldn't take it for free – they had to give him something in return. For every batch of soap he gave them, they left a bunch of rocks in his shed. By the time Dad told me and Mum about it, the shed was almost full.

'I don't know what to do,' he complained. 'I don't want to offend them, but I'm running out of room.'

'What kind of rocks are they, Dad?'

'Heavy ones.'

'All rocks are heavy, Dad. What colour?'

'Oh, I don't know. A rock colour, I suppose.'

Mum and Uncle Jeffrey and I went over to Dad's place to help him get rid of the rocks. Dad and Uncle Jeffrey had been getting along much better since they teamed up to rescue me. Dad was really happy to see us, and even happier to see Uncle Jeffrey's new trailer. I could see him calculating how many rocks would fit in it. Uncle Jeffrey knew some people who were landscaping their gardens, so he was going to give them some of the rocks for free. When Dad opened the shed door, rocks spilled out everywhere. Uncle Jeffrey picked up one of the smaller ones and held it to the light. All the colour drained out of his face.

'Jeff?' Mum asked. 'Is everything okay?'

'Martin,' Uncle Jeffrey said in a strange kind of voice. 'These rocks. They're gold, Martin. Gold! You're rich!'

CHAPTER 13

NOT OVER YET

It's the noise that wakes me. A noise that doesn't have any place in a house where everyone is asleep. I open my eyes slowly, straining my ears to catch the sound, but everything is still and quiet. I lie silently for a while, waiting. I can hear Billy's dad outside playing fetch with Killer, but that's all. Yawning, I close my eyes again. And that's when I hear it – 'BEEP! BEEP! BEEP!'

It's coming from outside. I jump out of
bed and head for the front door. When I
open it I find a giant truck backing into our
drive, and Dad sitting on the front lawn
wearing a Christmas hat.

'HO! HO! HO!' he shouts. 'What did I tell
you, Curly? A whole truckload of toys!'

Mum comes up behind me. 'Martin,
what have you done? I'll never fit it all in the
house!'

'That's all right, Jane,' Dad says with a sly
smile. 'I've bought you another one. It's a lot
bigger. And it has a swimming pool.'

Mum stares at him. I don't think she knows what to say. I wonder if Dad's bought Uncle Jeffrey something too. In my mind I picture a car yard.

Dad grins at me. 'That's right, Curly!' he says. 'That's dead right! I bought him an entire fleet of cars! Red cars!'

And that's when I hear a small voice chirping in my ear. 'Hehehe. I like red cars, Curly. I like them a *lot*.'

The trouble isn't over yet!

Keep reading for a special preview
of book two in the Curly series:

CURLY
SAVES GRANDMA'S
HOUSE

CHAPTER 1

ANY-THING?

'What are you going to dream tonight, Curly?'

It's late. Pook is tucked in his little bed inside my wardrobe, but he *still* wants to talk!

'I'm not dreaming anything. I'm just sleeping!'

I spent all day at a community Christmas party, giving away most of the toys Dad had bought me with the money he made from selling his edible soap to the Fents. I'm exhausted from having fun.

'What am I going to dream tonight, then, Curly?'

'How would I know? Go to sleep! Uncle Jeffrey's picking us up early. Remember?'

'The Red Racer!' he chirps in delight. The Red Racer is Uncle Jeffrey's new sports car. 'I like it, Curly. I like it a *lot!*'

'I like it too, but it'll get here faster if you go to sleep!'

'Don't worry, Curly, I'll put you in my dream.'

'Okay,' I mutter, dropping off to sleep. 'Thanks.'

I'm hurtling along at breakneck speed in the Red Racer.

'SLOW DOWN!' I scream at Pook.

He jerks the steering wheel to the left. We veer off the road, fly down an embankment and race towards a giant gum tree.

'BRAKE!'

Pook grins. 'Break what?'

I fling myself in front of Pook's feathered feet and slam my hand hard on the brake pedal. The car spins, then somersaults through the air, shuddering to a bone-jarring halt at the base of the tree.

'Curly's a hero! Curly's a hero!' Pook cheers.

My eyes fly open in shock. I'm tangled in my bed sheets and covered in sweat.

'Did you like it?' Pook grins, bouncing up and down on my chest. Daylight is pouring in through the window. It's morning already.

'L-l-like what?'

'The dream I put you in.'

'*You* did that?'

He nods. 'I made you a hero!'

'Don't ever make me a hero again!'

'Hehehe!' he laughs, then vanishes into thin air.

Mum bangs on the door. 'Uncle Jeffrey will be here soon, boys.'

I've slept in! Unwinding myself from the sheets, I leap out of bed and throw on a pair of shorts and a T-shirt.

'Let's play Hide and Seek,' Pook urges, reappearing with my backpack in his hands.

'No!' I'm still mad about the dream. I grab my backpack off him and shove some clothes inside.

'Just one game,' he pleads, making his eyes go big.

I hate it went he does that. I'm weakening already. I suppose it's too late for breakfast. And he *is* easy to find.

'Okay,' I agree.

I close my eyes and count to ten. Then I look under my bed, inside my wardrobe and behind my door. No Fent. I'm surprised. They're his favourite hiding places.

TOOT! TOOOT!

That's Uncle Jeffrey. We don't have time

for games any more.

'I give up, Pook! You win. Where are you?'

'Here!' he chirps triumphantly, magically appearing before me. 'I was hiding in the air, Curly!'

'That's not fair! We agreed, no magic!'

'We only agreed for *some* games. Not *all* of them!'

A lot of things have changed since Pook and I first met, but he's still *really* annoying.

I sling my backpack over my shoulder and tear outside.

'Don't be mad, Curly!' he yells, chasing me. 'It was just a trick.'

I dodge the kiss Mum tries to plant on my cheek, and leap into the car.

'No feet on the leather seat!' Uncle Jeffrey growls.

'Have a good time at your grandmother's, Curly,' Mum laughs.

Pook scrambles in on top of me and I shove him over the back. I'm sick of him cheating.

'Is your friend on board?' Uncle Jeffrey asks, looking around.

Adults can't see Fents. And despite everything that's happened, Uncle Jeffrey's still not positive they're real.

'He's in the back, Uncle Jeffrey.'

'Right, let's get this little beauty on the road then!'

The Red Racer's engine revs loudly. With a sharp squeal of tyres we reverse out of the drive.

'Wheee!' Pook cries, as he's flung back in his seat. It's just as well I've taught him to wear a seatbelt.

We zoom around the corner, but as soon as we're out of sight of Mum, Uncle Jeffrey slows down.

'That's called showing off, Curly. Don't ever let me see you do that when you're my age!'

'I want to stay with Uncle Jeffrey,' Pook

chirps. 'He likes tricks!'

I don't want to stay with Uncle Jeffrey. Grandma might not have a television set or any computer games, but she's not even half as grumpy as he is.

'Your dad gave me a message for you, Curly,' Uncle Jeffrey says, as we turn onto the main highway. 'He said to tell you that your grandmother has a few things on her mind, so be really, really nice to her.'

Dad is away at an Inventors convention. He's trying to sell something called Eternal Oil to the automotive industry.

'What kind of things?'

'Knowing your dad's side of the family, it could be anything.'

'Anything?' Pook asks curiously. 'Any*thing*?'

I turn and look at his excited face. He's right! It could be any*thing*!

Maybe Grandma's won't be so boring after all!

Look out for

CURLY

SAVES GRANDMA'S

HOUSE

at your local bookshop
in early 2009

ABOUT THE AUTHORS

Ambelin Kwaymullina was born in 1975 in Perth. She is a Lecturer in the Law School at the University of Western Australia. When she is not teaching and writing she enjoys making jewellery, reading and taking her two dogs Tinsel and Sparky for long, interesting walks.

Blaze Kwaymullina was born in 1978 in Perth. He is a Lecturer in the School of Indigenous Studies at the University of Western Australia. Blaze is interested in reading, rock climbing, yoga and taking his two dogs Chris and Billy swimming at the local dog beach.

Ezekiel Kwaymullina was born in 1983 in Perth. He writes full time. Zeke loves beach walking, soccer, basketball, computer games, reading and hanging out with his friends.

Sally Morgan was born in 1951 in Perth. She works at the School of Indigenous Studies at the University of Western Australia. Sally loves painting pictures, reading, beach walking and collecting junk for car boot sales.

Ambelin's picture book *Crow and the Waterhole* was published in 2007 and *The Two-Hearted Numbat* by Ambelin and Ezekiel will be published in 2008. Sally has written fiction and non-fiction for children and adults. Her children's books include *Dan's Grandpa*, *The Little Brown Dog* and *The Flying Emu and Other Australian Stories*. Her biography, *My Place*, has also been published in a children's edition, *Sally's Story*. Together with Tjalaminua Mia, Sally and Blaze have edited two collections of non-fiction, *Speaking from the Heart: stories of life, family and country* and *Heartsick for Country: stories of love, spirit and creation*.

Sally, Ambelin, Blaze and Zeke are descendants of the Palkyu people of the Pilbara in the north-west of Western Australia.

WRITING CURLY AND THE FENT

Sally, Ambelin, Blaze and Ezekiel enjoy putting their creative skills together to invent wacky ideas for new stories. This involves a great deal of imagining, arguing and playing around with silly thoughts and suggestions, until they find the right one for the right story. They also take notice of their dreams. Sometimes the ideas or images that come to them in dreams are used in their stories. They hope to spend the rest of their lives writing stories that children enjoy reading. They would be very pleased to hear from any children interested in story writing.

ABOUT THE ILLUSTRATOR

Adam Hill is a Dhungatti Aboriginal descendant. He's a painter, graphic designer, illustrator and cartoonist. Adam is a multi-award-winner in the medium of acrylic on canvas, and his public artworks and murals have adorned the walls of schools, council structures and shopping malls. Most recently Adam has illustrated *Yirra and Her Deadly Dog, Demon* by Anita Heiss. Adam is also an accomplished performer of Yidaki (Didgeridoo), and has performed for Nelson Mandela and at the Deadly Awards, the Rugby World Cup opening ceremony and the final of *Australian Idol*.